Tweenies™

I'm not scared

BBC

Bella, Milo, Fizz and Jake were having a lovely time, dancing to one of their favourite songs.

"You know you have a friend when they dance with you.
You have to choose a partner, 'cos it's better with two.

You have to spin
your partner,
that's what you do.
W-H-E-E-E-E-E!"

Giggling and laughing,
they spun all over the room.
"Who-aaa!" giggled Jake as
he swayed backwards
and forwards by the curtain.

Suddenly he heard a noise that made him **jump!**

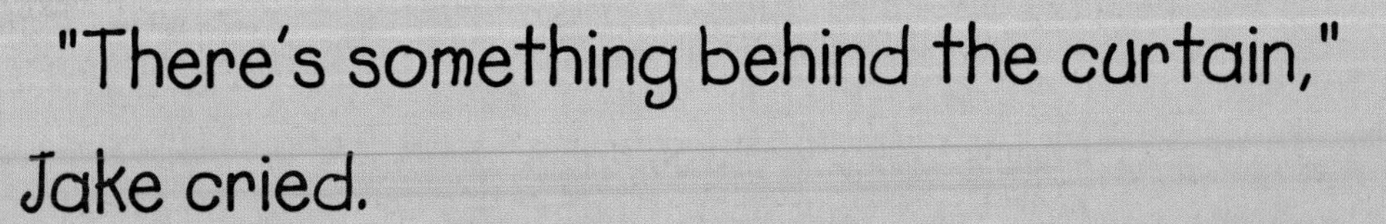

"There's something behind the curtain," Jake cried.

"No, there isn't," said Milo. "You're imagining it."

"I really did hear something," Jake insisted.

He crept right up to the curtain. Just then the curtain began to twitch.

"Arghhh! The curtain's moving!" he yelled.

"You're just trying to scare us," said Bella.

"There really really is something there," said Jake shakily.

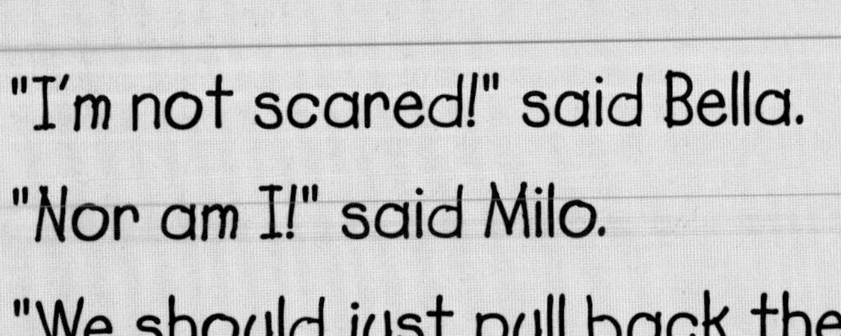

"I'm not scared!" said Bella.

"Nor am I!" said Milo.

"We should just pull back the curtain!" said Bella.

"Go on then, Bella," urged Milo.

"Why ME?" cried Bella.

"You're the oldest - and you said you weren't scared," Milo reminded her.

Bella crept slowly forwards, but the curtain moved again. She screamed and ran away.

"Do you think it's Max playing a trick on us?" asked Jake.

"Let's see," said Fizz. She was about to peep behind the curtain when she heard a grunting noise.

"Arghhhhh," she yelled!

The Tweenies rushed off to hide.

"There's something over there," Jake whispered. "But I'm not scared, not me!" The Tweenies decided to sing a special song to feel brave.

There's something, something over there.
But I'm not scared - no, I'm not scared.
There's something, something over there.
But I'm not scared - not me!

I hope that it's a monkey,
a monkey, a monkey.
I hope that it's a monkey
that wants to swing with me.

I hope that it's a teddy,
a teddy, a teddy.
I hope that it's a teddy that
wants to dance with me.

I hope that it's a spaceman,
a spaceman, a spaceman.
I hope that it's a spaceman
who's come to visit me.

I hope that it's a fairy,
a fairy, a fairy.
I hope that it's a fairy
to put a spell on me!

There's something, something over there.
But I'm not scared - no, I'm not scared.
There's something, something over there.
But I'm not scared - not me!

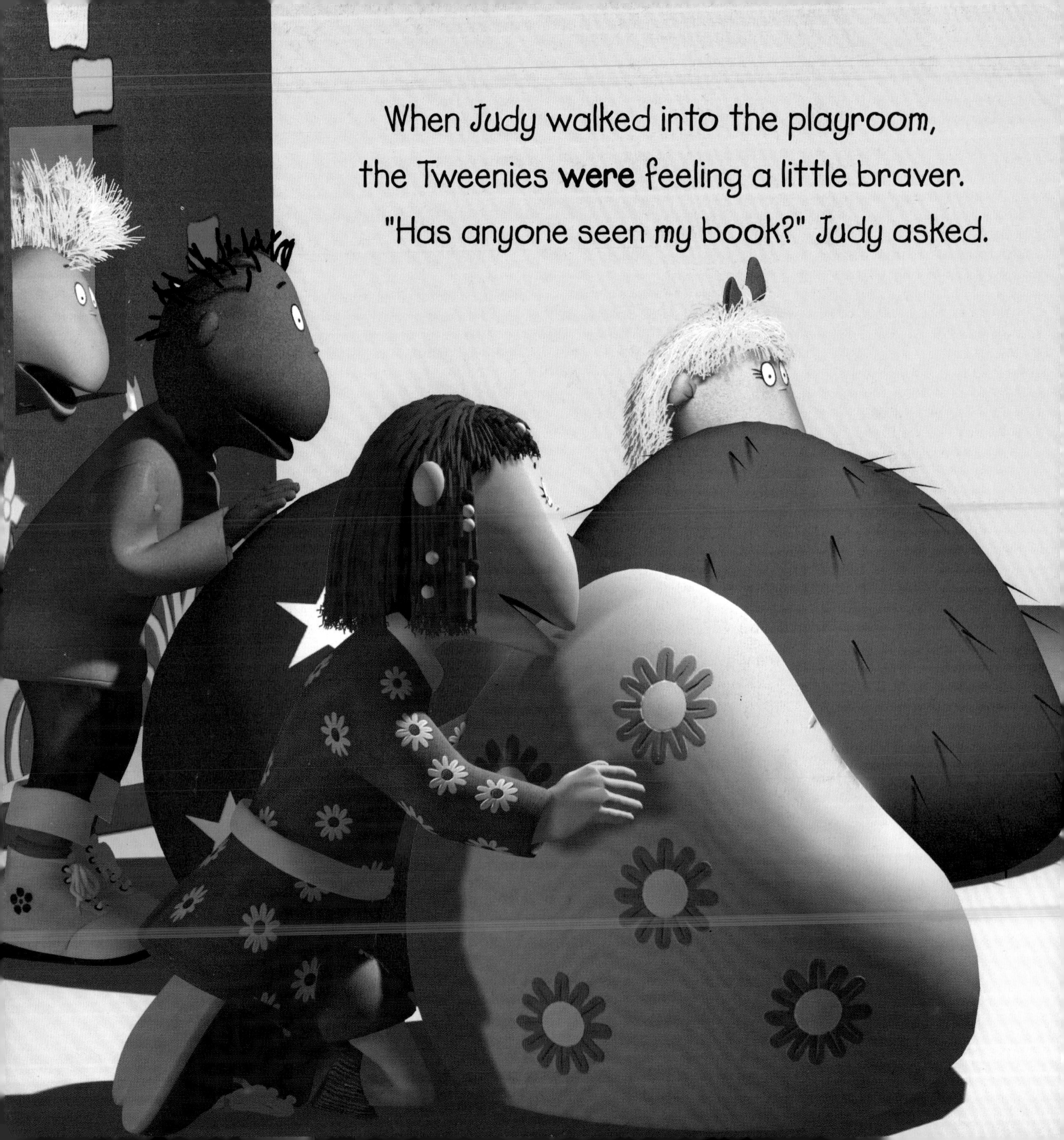

When Judy walked into the playroom, the Tweenies **were** feeling a little braver.

"Has anyone seen *my* book?" Judy asked.

The Tweenies shook their heads. But when Judy walked over to the curtain, they began to feel scared all over again.

"ARGHHHH!" they gasped.

Judy reached behind the curtain...

and brought out a book!
She settled down in the book corner and the Tweenies snuggled up to her.

"Did you see anything behind the curtain," Milo asked.

"Yes," said Judy.

Fizz, Milo, Jake and Bella gulped.

"WHAT did you see?" squeaked Fizz."

"I saw a great, big, hairy thing," said Judy.

"Arghhhhhh!" squeaked Jake. "Has it got TEN eyes and EIGHT legs?" Judy smiled and shook her head. "No, it's got two eyes and four legs, and it's very friendly."

"Are you sure it's friendly?" asked Fizz.

"I'm very, very sure," Judy replied. "Go and see for yourself. Don't worry. I'll be right here."

The Tweenies crept

very

very

slowly

up to the curtain.

"I'll count to three and we'll all pull together," Bella whispered.

"ONE,

TWO,

THREE,

PULL!"

"It's DOODLES!"

cried Jake. "Oh, I'm **so** glad to see you, Doodles."

"We're not scared of Doodles," giggled Fizz.

SNUFFLE
SPLUTTER
GRUNT

Doodles woke up and wagged his tail.
"Woof! Woof!" he barked.

THE END